Baby Bunny's Birthday

By

Elizabeth Marie Stanhope

For Magdalena

Baby Bunny's Birthday

Far away, deep in the woods, lives the Bunny Family.

Today is a SPECIAL DAY. It is Baby Bunny's Birthday!

"What do you want for your birthday, Baby Bunny?"

"A Picnic!"

"What a good idea!" said Mummy Bunny. She smiled at Daddy Bunny.

"I'll get the picnic basket." Said Daddy Bunny

"What shall we have for the picnic?" said Baby Bunny.

"It's a surprise!"

said Daddy Bunny

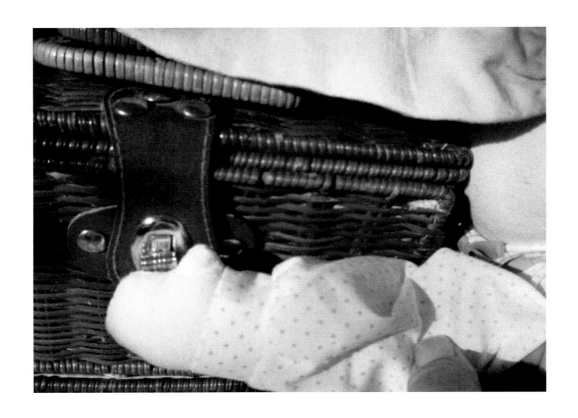

Daddy Bunny opened the picnic basket

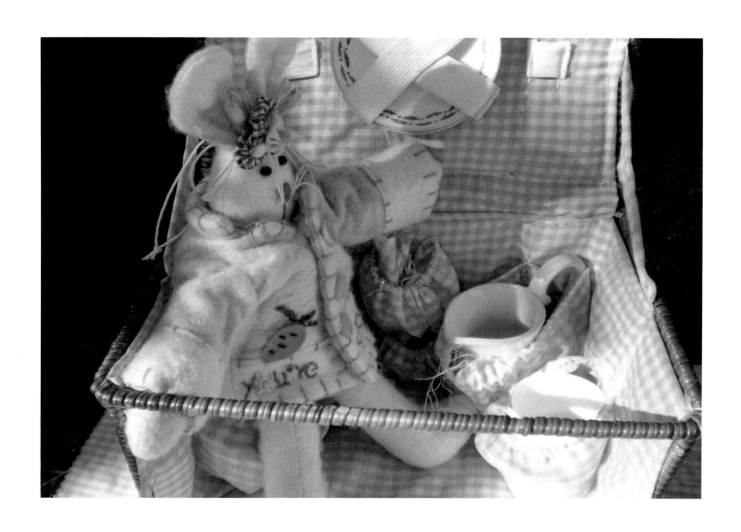

"I love surprises!" said Baby Bunny, and jumped into the picnic basket

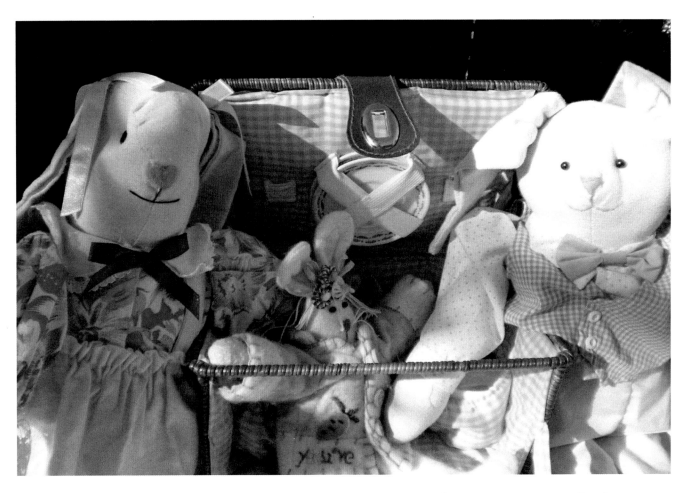

Daddy and Mummy Bunny laughed – "Come on out, Baby Bunny," they said.

Time to set up the picnic.

Daddy Bunny set the table.

Baby Bunny helped.

But where's Brother Bunny?

Surprise!

Carrots for everyone!

Brother Bunny gave Baby Bunny the first carrot.

And they ate them all. What a lovely picnic.

"Time to go home" said Daddy Bunny.

So they did.

"Time for bed, Baby Bunny. Did you have a nice birthday?

Made in the USA
Las Vegas, NV
06 July 2021